Climbing Sun

Climbing Sun

The Story of a Hopi Indian Boy

MARJORIE THAYER &
ELIZABETH EMANUEL
Woodcuts by Anne Siberell

DODD, MEAD & COMPANY   NEW YORK

To JAD

Library of Congress Cataloging in Publication Data

Thayer, Marjorie.
Climbing Sun.

SUMMARY: In the fall of 1928 an 11-year-old Indian
boy leaves his Hopi village on the mesa and travels by
train to the Sherman Indian Institute where he will
learn the white man's ways.
1.   Honanie, Hubert—Juvenile fiction.
[1.   Honanie, Hubert—Fiction.   2.   Hopi Indians—
Fiction.   3.   Indians of North America—Fiction]
I.   Emanuel, Elizabeth, joint author.   II.   Siberell,
Anne.   III.   Title.
PZ7.T3299Cl   [Fic]   80–13743
ISBN 0–396–07844–3

Foreword

We first met the hero of *Climbing Sun* one October afternoon in 1977. He was standing in the sunny doorway to his workshop, a broad smile of welcome lighting up his handsome bronzed face. We had learned of Hubert Honanie from Dr. Carl Dentzel, curator of California's Southwest Museum. A distinguished Hopi Indian, Dr. Dentzel had told us that Honanie was known far and wide as the maker of authentic Kachina dolls. He also enjoyed an enviable reputation as a cabinetmaker and restorer of fine furniture.

The carved and painted Kachina dolls we saw that day were indeed wonderful but, as our visit progressed, and in answer to our many questions, it was the glimpses we caught of this modern Hopi's early life—his boyhood spent on a Hopi reservation in northeastern Arizona and at Sherman Indian School in Riverside, California—that most captured our attention. Here was the story of a boyhood lived in two different worlds, the Hopi's, little changed in many centuries, and the white man's world of school where the Indian was compelled to exchange his language, his traditions, his daily way of life for another way, completely alien to him. Here was conflict, the basis of a good story.

And so, through many illuminating and always interesting conversations with Hubert Honanie, *Climbing Sun* gradually began to evolve. Hubert had first left his reservation to attend Sherman Indian Institute (as it was then called) in 1928 at age eleven. Since that time, the direction and shape of compulsory education of the American Indian has greatly changed. Concerted effort to preserve, with respect, the Indians' heritage is now in effect, but the record of the past is still there.

Hubert Honanie's story has been fictionalized for readability. Many of the incidents and some of the characters have been invented; also, some names have been changed. However, the names of Hubert's brothers and sisters are the real ones, their Anglo names given them during their early school years. Chimopovy, the name of Hubert's village, was officially changed to Shongopovi in the 1930s.

Two years of research went into the writing of *Climbing Sun*. The authors wish to express their thanks and appreciation to the many individuals who gave invaluable help during this period, particularly staff members of the Southwest Museum in Los Angeles and the Los Angeles Public Library. Special thanks go to Ramona Bradley, curator of the Sherman Museum, for supplying valuable details and for patiently answering our many questions.

MARJORIE THAYER
ELIZABETH EMANUEL

Climbing Sun

1 The thing coming toward him down the shining, silver-colored tracks looked like a huge black monster. It seemed to have a long tail that swayed a little as it drew nearer. It let out a great cloud of white smoke. Suddenly, a sound like a shriek split the quiet of the autumn afternoon.

For all the determined set of his squared shoulders, the boy standing on the small wooden platform was deeply afraid. But he must not show it. He was Hubert Honanie, a Hopi Indian boy of eleven years. His Hopi name was Dawa-Wufto—Climbing Sun—but he had been called Hubert, the Anglo name his teachers had given him, ever since his first day four years ago at the little Anglo day school at the foot of the mesa.

The black monster was coming nearer now, still puffing smoke. Of course Hubert knew that it was not really a monster. It was a train—a train which, in a few moments, would carry him miles away from all the life he knew into a strange new world, the world of the white man's ways.

Hubert glanced at his sister Janet standing beside him. She was busy talking to Mr. Downing, the day school teacher who, that morning, had driven them in his car from the Hopi village of Chimopovy on the Second Mesa to Flagstaff to catch this train which would take them to Riverside, California, and to Sherman Indian Institute. Janet could not be expected to feel this fear which seemed to lodge somewhere near the middle of Hubert's stomach. After all, his sister was fifteen and had gone away to Sherman each year for the last four years. Soon she would be through high school there. Hubert was comforted that he would be making this strange journey with her.

The great shrieking monster had come to a halt beside the small wooden station with its painted sign reading FLAGSTAFF, ARIZONA. It was quiet now, but from its sides issued billows of grayish-white steam. The late afternoon sun slanted across the platform, making prisms of light.

Mr. Downing turned away from Janet and spoke to Hubert. "Well, my boy," he said, a smile lighting up his usually solemn face, "you are about to make the big leap. Sherman Institute will be pretty different from our little school down below the mesa. Eh, Janet?"

Janet grinned back. "I've already told Hubert," she said.

"And I've told him he'd better stay out of trouble because I won't be around to help him if he gets into any. The girls' dorms are way off from the boys'. I won't see him much, except maybe on Sundays."

Mr. Downing nodded. "Hubert won't get into trouble. He's a good boy. Most of the time," he added, with a twinkle at Hubert. "Study hard, obey the rules, and you'll do fine. Remember that the education you get at Sherman is a great opportunity for you."

"*All aboard!*" The call came from the uniformed white man standing beside the train.

"Okay, Hubert," Janet said. "This is it. Say good-bye to Mr. Downing and thank him for the ride. Here we go!"

Hubert gulped a quick "Thank you" and followed his sister up the three steps of the first passenger car. The long boxlike room in which he suddenly found himself was like nothing he had ever seen before. There were two rows of cloth-covered seats, beside them big windows covered with glass. Through one of them he could see Mr. Downing still standing on the platform. The car gave a sudden lurch, which made him stumble. He bumped into Janet walking ahead of him.

"Watch it, stupid," she said crossly. "We'll sit here." She deposited the willow basket she was carrying on the seat. Then she took hold of the back of the seat directly in front of it and gave it a jerk. To Hubert's surprise, it moved, slid back—and there were two seats facing one another, with space between. "You ride backward," Janet said. "After while maybe we'll change off."

Hubert sat down facing Janet. He looked around him at the other passengers. Some were occupying seats; others, new arrivals, were walking down the aisle looking for places. Most of them were Anglos, with here and there a scattering of Indians. Some of the Indians wore blankets.

Hubert looked down at his own clothes. They were new, put on early that morning. Mr. Downing had brought them when he came to make arrangements to drive Hubert and Janet to Flagstaff. Blue cotton pants, a plaid shirt, and heavy low shoes. The Government had paid for them, Mr. Downing said. Hubert would be given his school clothes—a uniform (whatever that was)—when he reached Sherman. Mr. Downing said it was best that he take nothing with him from his home on the mesa.

The train began to move, slowly at first. The station and the low buildings next to it began to slide away. Then the train picked up speed. Soon they were moving through a pine forest, the tall trees seeming to tower above them. In the distance Hubert could see the mountains, blue in the fading afternoon sunlight. These were the San Francisco Mountains where the Spirit World Kachinas, the messengers to the Hopi gods, were said to live. He looked over at Janet. She was reading a magazine, not even bothering to glance out the window. She would be cross if he interrupted her.

It had been a long day and Hubert was beginning to feel sleepy. Perhaps he would sleep a little. After that he would ask Janet to open up the basket so that he could have some of the good piki bread and the mutton their older sister Rachel had packed for them.

He leaned his head back against the rough covering of the seat and closed his eyes. But he found that he was more wide awake than he thought. There was too much to think about for sleep. He tried to picture to himself what this new school would be like. He knew that Rachel and his big brother Perry had been there before Janet, but when they came back to the village for vacations they never said much about Sherman. He wouldn't have listened to them anyway. He hadn't been interested in school.

His thoughts traveled back to early morning of this day. The sun was just beginning to climb over the edge of the mesa when he had wakened. Someone was shaking him by the shoulder. "Get up, my son," his father's voice said. "Mr. Downing will be here within the hour. Hurry and get ready. You must eat something before you go."

Hubert had crawled out from under the sheepskin on the floor in which he had been wrapped. He got to his feet. Half awake, his father's words meant little to him. At first he thought that it must be time to go down the trail to the cornfield. Then, with a jolt, he remembered. School! But this time a school miles and miles—hundreds of miles—away. Tomorrow he would not wake up to the four walls of the stone house on the Second Mesa—the house where he and his brothers and sisters had been born and had grown up.

School—the white man's school! That was what had caused all the trouble he had known in his short life. This day had begun like that other one four years ago. Though he was only seven then, he remembered it in sharp detail. That day it was Grandfather Honanie who had wakened him as he slept on the floor, curled up in a tight ball like a porcupine. At first he hadn't understood what was happening to him. That time, too, he had thought that Grandfather must be taking him to the cornfield to help with the harvest.

Outside the house Grandfather had lifted him onto the back of the little burro they used for journeys down the steep side of the cliff to the valley below. But it was not to the cornfield they went in the early morning light. Instead, Grandfather headed the burro toward the small one-story wooden building sitting by itself under a cluster of fruit trees.

The schoolhouse! He had heard of this school from his older brothers and sisters who had been there, but he had paid little attention to anything they had said about it. Now he sat up straighter, filled with dread. He was going to be made to go to this white man's school.

A few children were playing tag in the dusty yard which surrounded the building. A tall man dressed in dark Anglo clothes stood in the doorway. He raised a hand in greeting. "Well, so here is another Honanie come to school," the man said to Grandfather.

"This is my grandson, Dawa-Wufto," Grandfather answered.

"Welcome to Chimopovy Day School," the man said to Hubert. "My name is Mr. Downing. My wife and I are the teachers here." He looked carefully at Hubert and frowned. "Before school begins today, though, we'd better clean you up!"

Before he really knew what was happening to him, Hubert was being pushed inside, into a big room which, he learned later, was the laundry. In the center of the room was a big tin tub. Mr. Downing quickly pulled off his pants, then his shirt—and plunged him over the tub's side into cold, soapy water! Hubert yelled loudly—but worse was yet to come. After Mr. Downing had scrubbed him, then dried him with a big towel, he gave him a clean shirt and a pair of baggy overalls to put on, sat him down on a box near the tub—and cut his hair!

His long black hair which hung straight, nearly to his shoulders, fell away. Now his hair was trimmed Anglo-style, short above his ears, with bangs across his forehead.

"Stop howling," Mr. Downing said sharply, giving Hubert's shoulder a shake. "Behave yourself. It's time for school to begin. Everybody gets a scrubbing and a haircut when they come to school. You should know that," he added impatiently.

In the schoolroom a white lady, Mrs. Downing, who was as round and fat as her husband was tall and thin, was

15

writing on the blackboard in big letters with white chalk. The Hopi children from the mesa village, many of whom Hubert recognized, were sitting on wooden benches behind funny-looking tables.

Mr. Downing began to speak in the Anglo language. He had used Hopi before, but now Hubert couldn't understand what he was saying. He gathered it had something to do with the words Mrs. Downing was writing on the blackboard. She kept pointing to them with a long stick as her husband talked.

The boy sitting next to Hubert whispered to him in Hopi. "We're going to choose our Anglo names in a minute. Everyone new has to choose one. Pick out the one you want from up there and yell it out."

Suddenly everybody seemed to be talking at once. Boys and girls around him were shouting out strange words— "Kathleen, John, Harry, Mary, Peter . . ." Mrs. Downing was crossing out words as the children shouted.

Hubert sat silent, dumb with confusion. The voices died down. Mrs. Downing was looking directly at him. She pointed at him with her long stick, then to a word on the blackboard—the only word not yet crossed out. "Hubert," she said. "It's the only name left. From now on you will be called Hubert Honanie."

At last it was recess, time to go outside and play for a few minutes. Tom, a boy a little older than Hubert, with whom he had sometimes spun tops of an afternoon in the village plaza, explained to him what had happened. "Everybody has to have an Anglo name," he said. "That's how I got the name Tom. No more Hopi names, or Hopi words either. Here you have to speak Anglo all the time. If you speak Hopi, they beat you!"

In a little while Mr. Downing called them back inside. Hubert slid quietly into his seat. Hubert! What a name! What did it mean? He was Dawa-Wufto, Climbing Sun, the name given to him at dawn of his Naming Day when he was just three weeks old. His mother and his grandmother had held him up to the rising sun as it sent its first light over the edge of the mesa. Climbing Sun—a name to be proud of, not this silly-sounding, meaningless white man's name.

The rest of the day passed in a kind of dream. The "new" Hubert understood almost nothing of what went on around him. He shrank farther and farther down in his seat, trying, as nearly as possible, to make himself invisible. But at last the day was over. Mrs. Downing rang a little bell on her desk and told them all they could go home.

With loud squeals and cries, the children stormed the schoolhouse door, Hubert among them. Never had he scrambled up the stony cliff path so eagerly. Never had the village and home looked so desirable.

Later in the afternoon, shed of the baggy overalls and shirt the white man had dressed him in, clad only in the ragged short pants he was accustomed to wear and carrying his slingshot, he hurried past the boys who were spinning tops in the middle of the plaza, down the cliff trail once more. He didn't want to play with anybody. He would go into the fields and get a rabbit for supper tonight. At least his family would be proud of him. But he was disappointed. He saw only one rabbit and it disappeared before he could get near enough to take aim.

That night after the evening meal he sought out Grandfather. The old man was sitting cross-legged in the doorway of his house which adjoined the house of Hubert's family. He was smoking his evening pipe.

"Grandfather," Hubert said, "tell me why I have to go to the Anglo school instead of helping you and my father in the fields. I have no need of the white man's language. In that school we cannot speak in Hopi. The teachers will beat us if we do! Why, Grandfather, *why?*"

Grandfather puffed on his pipe. The blue smoke curled upward in the still evening air. For a moment he did not speak. Then he said slowly, "My grandson, as you grow older you will learn many things that are hard to understand, but as you grow some things will become clear to you. This much I will tell you now, young as you are. Ever since he settled it a long time ago, the world has belonged to the white man. This land we Hopis live on, which the white man's law has given to us, is all we have left—the only place where we can live as our ancestors lived since the beginning. Since he came here as conqueror, the white man has wished us to live as he does. He has made it so that we must learn his language, use the Anglo names instead of our own. He has always tried to make us fit into his way of life and to give up our way."

18

Grandfather paused and shook his head sadly. "You must do what your white teachers will tell you, Dawa-Wufto—Climbing Sun. You must learn what they give you to learn. It is the only way. But, as you grow in years, no matter where you go or how hard it is for you, you must never forget that you are a Hopi, a Hopi with a proud name. Know this and be thankful for it."

2 "Wake up! It's time to eat." It was Janet's voice which roused him. Hubert looked outside the window of the train. It had grown dark. The train had crossed the mountains and was now speeding through flat desert country. Here and there, in the distance, clusters of lights shone from tiny villages in the vast spread of the desert.

Janet had opened up the willow basket. She handed Hubert some piki bread, the thin, waferlike baked corn bread that all Hopis prized. And there was some roasted corn too, along with a few slices of cold roast mutton. Hubert didn't know it then, but this supper was to be his last meal of Hopi food for a long time to come.

20

Other people throughout the car were eating from baskets, then settling down for the night. Hubert marveled at the lights shining overhead which had suddenly appeared in the ceiling like magic. Presently Janet showed him where the men's lavatory was. Its use, too, was a new and bewildering experience. When he came back, Janet was curled up in her seat, her eyes closed. He guessed that she was already asleep. The strange overhead lights above him had dimmed. Like Janet, most of the other passengers seemed asleep.

Hubert settled back and closed his eyes, but sleep would not come to him. His mind was still occupied with thoughts of Chimopovy. He thought about his mother, how she had died and how he had crawled away in the dark to cry. That had been a bad time which he did not like remembering. Now he was used to his sister Rachel looking after things. She was bossy sometimes, but he didn't really mind.

His thoughts wandered—to the biggest event in his life so far, his initiation into the Kachina Cult. It had happened in the late winter of this year, 1928, during the Powamu, the Bean-Growing Season. All Hopi children, boys and girls alike, were initiated into the Kachina Cult before they reached age twelve. The girls were not allowed to know its deeper mysteries, but the boys' initiation gave them full membership. From that time on they could participate in the Kachina dances that began in December each year and lasted until the Home-Going Ceremony in late July.

Now, with Sherman Institute looming ahead of him,

Hubert realized that he would be missing most of next year's activities. Instead of taking his rightful part in the Kachina dances, he would be learning how to live like a white man!

Like all Hopi children, Hubert had grown up with the Kachinas as a part of his life. Ever since he could remember, they had appeared in the cold of winter, a few of them at first, up out of the kivas, those great underground rooms deep within the earth. Dressed in elaborate masks and costumes, they were impressive and awe-inspiring.

The Kachinas, the Hopis believed, were not gods but the messengers to the gods. They were concerned with each Hopi's well-being, his health and happiness and long life. They understood the people's need for rain to insure growth and good crops. They disciplined the children, giving them lessons in proper behavior, and they gave them presents. Day after day they entertained everybody with their marvelous dances and their songs, some ancient, some new each year. In July, after the Home-Going Ceremony, they disappeared. It was believed that they returned to the faraway San Francisco Mountains, carrying with them the people's petitions to the gods for rain and good crops.

Hubert peered through the train window into the darkness. He could remember in vivid detail all that had happened the momentous day of his initiation. His father and his two uncles—his mother's brothers who were his sponsors—had led him, solemn-faced, into the kiva. He had been there many times before, in the company of his father or his grandfather, and had listened to the men's talk as they leaned against the kiva's walls, gossiping and smoking their pipes. But now it all looked formal and strange, with the altar, the sand painting on the floor, the trays holding the *pahos*, the sacred prayer sticks, and the ceremonial cornmeal. Most of all, the solemn movements of the masked Kachinas and their assistants as they went about their preparations struck terror to his heart. Hubert had heard about the initiation ceremony from some of the older boys, but they would not reveal details. They acted superior and said he would find out soon enough.

Many of his friends were already there. Some of the little girls were crying. All of the children, even the boys, looked frightened.

Soon a hush descended upon the entire room. Everyone turned to face the entrance to the kiva. Down the ladder that led into the room came the mysterious creature known as Crow Mother, the most important figure in the initiation rites, accompanied by the two Whipping Kachinas. Very tall and dressed all in black, with a white cloak trimmed in green, Crow Mother was an awesome presence. The mask was of blue with two black wings on either side. But it was what Crow Mother carried that was so frightening—a large bundle of yucca blades, bound together at the ends. This was the whip that soon would fall across the backs of each initiate.

Crow Mother took the appointed place at one corner of the sand painting, the Whipping Kachinas on either side. One by one the children were brought forward. The whip was handed to the Whipping Kachinas in turn. As the blows fell, most of the children cried out, though all had been told beforehand that this must be done, in order to cleanse them of past misbehavior. Without this cleansing it would be impossible to enter into membership in the Kachina Cult.

Hubert was determined not to cry. When his turn came he clenched his teeth hard. He made no sound, but he could not hold back the tears that suddenly stung his closed eyelids.

3 A shaft of bright sunlight coming through the window beside him wakened Hubert. He sat up. The seat opposite him was empty—Janet wasn't there! The awful feeling in the pit of his stomach which had been with him all day yesterday gripped him now with full force. They had come to Riverside and Janet had gotten off this train! She had forgotten him.

He looked out the window. The land was flat. Row after row of trees with shiny green leaves sparkled in the bright sunlight. Where was he? What was he to do?

Then he saw Janet sauntering down the aisle toward him. She grinned at him as she took her seat. "Well, sleepyhead," she said, "it's about time you woke up. We'll be at Riverside in a few minutes. Go wash your face and comb your hair. You look terrible."

"Riverside! Riverside!" a uniformed man was calling as he walked briskly down the aisle of the car. Hubert nearly bumped into him as he came out the door of the men's room. Hubert made a dive toward Janet. She was calmly gathering up the willow basket and the remains of the supper they had eaten last night. "Here," she said, thrusting a piece of piki bread toward him. "Eat this fast. It's all you'll get for quite awhile. And pull your shirt down. You look terrible!"

The next thing Hubert knew, they were standing outside on a low platform, surrounded by other travelers who had gotten off the train. Hubert was surprised to see that several of them were Indian boys and girls, some of them Hopis of about his own age. He hadn't seen any of them on the train. They must have been sitting in the other cars. To Hubert they all looked confident, self-assured, not scared.

Hubert looked back at the train standing beside them. Its engine was puffing and snorting, just as it had yesterday at the station in Flagstaff. He realized that he wasn't afraid of it any more. He squared his shoulders.

There was a confusion of sounds as people fumbled over strange-looking boxes and bags that had been set down on the platform. Most of the Indian boys and girls moved toward each other, grinning at one another. Then a loud voice called, "Sherman students over here. Everybody going to Sherman Institute step over here!"

26

A tall man in a jacket and pullover sweater was waving a long arm toward the crowd. "I'm Mr. Barton," he said, as soon as a little knot of Indian youngsters had gathered. "I'm here to meet you and to drive you out to the school. Welcome, everybody! Just follow me and the old bus will get you there in nothing flat."

Hubert followed Janet and the rest. Soon everybody was loaded into the wagonlike car with its upright seats. Hubert found himself scrunched in between two bigger boys who took up more room than he did. But he could see out a window. This town looked bigger than Flagstaff. Soon they were speeding down a broad street lined with strange-looking tall trees of a kind Hubert had never seen before. All the tree leaves seemed to grow at the very tops and waved in the breeze like giant fans. On either side of the street were low white houses with green grass growing around them. Then they were on a narrower road where there were only a few houses.

"Well, here we are," Mr. Barton said from the front seat.

The car turned off the road and followed a graveled driveway up to a high wire fence with a big gate. The gate swung open and Hubert saw a very large yard covered with grass. Surrounding the yard were many buildings painted a light brown. A tall pole stood in the middle of the yard and from it waved a red, white, and blue flag. Everywhere he looked he could see the strange leaf-topped tall trees.

Dozens of Indian boys and girls were walking about the yard or standing in small groups talking to each other. Hubert noticed that nearly all of them wore very odd-looking

27

clothes. The boys were dressed in dark blue long pants and dark blue jackets fastened as high as their chins. The girls wore dark skirts and stiff-looking white blouses. What surprised Hubert most was that everyone was dressed alike!

"All out, everybody," Mr. Barton said as the car drew up before one of the largest buildings. "The first thing you'll do is to find your dorm. For you new ones, I'll have somebody show you where to go. Later today we'll get you your uniforms." Hubert didn't understand what Mr. Barton was talking about but he got out of the car with the others, not daring to ask.

Janet had been sitting up in front near Mr. Barton. Now she turned to Hubert and smiled. "Well, so long, kid," she said to him. "I'll be seeing you. Stay out of trouble. If you get into any, don't expect me to help you out." She turned quickly and disappeared in the direction of one of the buildings.

Hubert stood still, feeling lost. Everybody else seemed to know what to do, where to go. But in a moment Mr. Barton was speaking to him. "What's your name, boy?" Hubert told him. Mr. Barton looked at a paper he was holding. "Oh, yes, here you are. You'll be in Hiawatha dorm. All our dormitories have Indian names. I'll get Frank to show you."

In another minute a boy, taller and older than Hubert, had joined them. "This is Frank Tawa, another Hopi. Frank comes from Oraibi," Mr. Barton said. "Frank, meet Hubert Honanie. Show him to his dorm—Hiawatha, Number 7. Look after him and see that he doesn't get lost. And make sure he gets to lunch on time."

Frank grinned at Hubert. "Well, kid, come along," he said. "I can see you're new around here all right. But don't look so scared. Nobody's going to eat you!"

Frank spoke in English and Hubert wasn't sure he understood all of his words. "Can't we talk in Hopi?" he asked timidly as they walked along. "I don't know much Anglo talk."

Frank rolled his eyes upward. "You must be kidding!" he exclaimed. "Don't you know it's a crime to talk anything but Anglo here? If they catch you talking Indian they grind you up and feed you to the pigs! And hurry up—I haven't got all day!"

Frank grabbed him by the elbow and hustled him toward one of the low brown buildings. Once inside, they walked down what seemed to be a long tunnel with doors on either side, then up some steps to the second floor. Here they turned into a large room filled with sunlight which streamed in through a doorway leading to a glassed-in porch outside. "Your bunk's on the porch," Frank was saying. "It's the upper one. Your locker's Number 7."

"Bunk? Locker?" Hubert repeated. "I do not understand," he added in Hopi.

"My gosh you're dumb!" Frank was frowning at him. "A bunk's a bed—where you sleep, dummy. That's yours, right over there. A locker's to keep your stuff in. And you'd better keep it there too. They kill you if you're not neat."

As Hubert stared around him a shrill, high sound seemed

to pierce the air. It filled his ears and echoed in his head.

"It's only the bell, stupid." Frank was laughing at him. "That one's telling us it's time for lunch. We live by bells here—you'll find out. Come along now! You don't want to be late your first day, do you? They shoot kids for being late."

Hubert knew that again Frank was only teasing him, but he hurried after him just the same. He realized all at once that he was ravenously hungry.

But in the large dining hall with its row after row of Indian boys and girls seated at long tables, he had no appetite for the strange food set before him. The main dish was something that tasted horrible. It was called hash, Frank told him. He thought longingly of the Middle-of-the-Sun meal at home, of rabbit stew and the piki bread Rachel would have baked. Everybody around him was talking in English. He understood only a little of what they said.

While they ate this strange meal, Hubert had a chance to look around him. He looked eagerly for Janet. At last he saw her, at a table halfway across the hall, talking away to some other girls. She was laughing as if at some joke. She did not glance in his direction. She had already forgotten him.

Except for the Anglo teachers, everyone in the hall was Indian. But not everyone was Hopi. Many of the boys, and the girls too, were thin and tall, taller than Hopis, with sharp features, not soft and round like Hopi faces were. Hubert remembered now what Mr. Downing had said—

that there would be Indians of many tribes from all over the Southwest at Sherman—Navajos, Cheyennes, Paiutes, Zunis, Papagos, Havasupais. As he thought about this, he began to feel more lonely than ever.

The rest of the day passed swiftly. Hubert could not remember afterward all that had happened, at least not clearly. After lunch was over everybody had been herded into a very large room in another building, a room which, Frank told him, was called the auditorium. There a short man with gray hair who, he said, was Superintendent of Sherman Institute, made a speech. He said that everybody was welcome, especially the newcomers; that he hoped everyone would settle down and study very hard; that the purpose of the school was to fit Indian boys and girls for life in the white man's world so that they could earn a living and enjoy the good things the white man's world offered. He said much more, a lot of which Hubert could not follow.

Then came the business of getting enrolled and assigned to classes which would begin in the morning. Hubert had finished four years of school at Chimopovy and so would enter the fifth grade.

Next, he was being given dark blue pants and a jacket to wear, like the clothes he had first seen the other boys wearing when he arrived. He stood in line to get them. They were being handed out by a white lady who measured each boy in turn. The clothes, she told Hubert, were called a uniform and were provided by the United States Government. They meant that he was now a student at Sherman

Indian Institute. In them, the lady said, he would learn to march and to drill on the Parade Ground, the big yard outside. The uniform made him almost a soldier, she said.

Hubert was not sure whether this was good or bad. He did not feel comfortable in the new clothes when he tried them on. The jacket had many shiny brass buttons down the front. The high stand-up collar was stiff. He must take care that it did not choke him. He did not dare to try to remember how it had felt to wear only ragged knee pants and to run free on the mesa.

4 Something was hammering inside Hubert's head. Demons were after him, pulling at his ears. His eyes still shut tight, he sat up. The fearsome sound continued. He opened his eyes. It was daylight on the porch where he had slept. He looked over the side of the bunk. The boy in the bed below was sitting up, stretching and yawning. Through the door that led inside Hubert could hear sounds, groans, then laughter. Suddenly he remembered. He was in a strange building called a dorm, in something called a bunk. The loud noise was the bell, telling him to get up.

Frank's head poked around the door opening onto the porch. "Get going, kid," he said. He was grinning. "Believe me, they skin you alive if you're late for breakfast!"

For Hubert this second day at Sherman seemed even more bewildering than the first. For one thing, most of the time he didn't have Frank, who was in an upper grade, to guide him. The boys and girls in the fifth grade room seemed friendly enough, and the teacher, Mr. Redmond, did not look too forbidding. It was the Anglo language, which everyone else seemed to know, that made it all so hard, so incomprehensible at times. Hubert wished with all his heart that he had tried to learn more English back at the day school at Chimopovy, that he had paid more attention to what the Downings had tried to teach him. Now he must study—language, reading, spelling, arithmetic, something called civics (whatever that was), geography, science—and all in English! This grade was going to be too hard for him!

It was midafternoon when the shrill sound of the bell, which still made Hubert jump every time it rang, finally signaled the end of the day's classes. At last he was free— free to do what he chose, at least for a little while. He was heading for the dorm when a voice behind him said, "Hey, kiddo, how're you doing? Taken any wooden nickels yet?" It was Frank, who laid a friendly hand on his shoulder. "Come on with me," he said. "It's time you saw our famous athletic field. Ever seen a football game? I bet you haven't. It's some game!"

Silently Hubert followed Frank across the Parade Ground toward a big stretch of bare land which lay be-

34

yond the school buildings. A game of some kind was in progress. Boys were tossing—or sometimes kicking—an oval-shaped ball at one another. When a boy caught the ball he tucked it under his arm and ran with it toward two upright poles with a pole between them that stood at each end of the field. The other boys ran after the one with the ball, as hard as they could. If they caught up with him before he reached the poles, they grabbed him and threw him to the ground, piling up on top of him. There were two white men on the field who ran about too. Now and then they blew whistles and shouted at the players.

Hubert, following Frank who had elbowed his way through the crowd of boys watching the game, stood with him very near to the players. He never knew exactly how it happened, but all of a sudden the oval ball was coming his way, hurtling through the air. Almost without thinking, Hubert put up his arms and caught it, then hugged it against his chest. For a second he stood there, stupidly. Boys around him were yelling. He heard the word "Run!"

Instead of dropping the ball, Hubert ran. Just where he was running to, or why, he wasn't sure. But running felt good. His legs stretched, his feet pounded on the turf. The air streamed past him. It was almost like running a race on the mesa top. Feet pounded behind him. Voices were shouting. He turned his head, just a little. Behind him, almost up to him, was a boy who was outdistancing the others. His face was contorted by a fierce scowl. He looked very angry.

Ahead loomed those strange upright poles with the pole between them. Hubert knew he must reach them before the boy caught up with him. He made one last effort, the ball still clutched against his chest. His pursuer was nearly up to him, his arms outstretched to grab him and hold him back. With a mighty effort, Hubert speeded up. He was almost there. With a burst of speed he passed between the two poles.

The crowd of runners who had followed him came pounding up. Most of them were laughing. But the boy who had nearly caught him was not laughing. He looked furiously angry. "You idiot!" he said between his teeth. "Don't you know any better than to catch the ball when you're only watching from the sideline? That pass was meant for *me!* I ought to punch the daylights out of you. I ought to kill you!"

The white man with the whistle came up to them. "Knock it off, George," he said. "The kid's new around here." He turned to Hubert. "Is this the first time you've ever watched a football game?" he asked him. Bewildered, Hubert nodded. "I thought so," the man said. "Next time you watch, don't try to get into the game too. Besides, boy, you were running the wrong way!" Everybody laughed, except the boy called George.

The man looked Hubert over speculatively. "Where did you learn to run like that?" he asked. "You'd better try out for the track team. We could use you in the 220. What's your name?" Hubert told him. The man nodded and turned to the players who were still laughing. "Break it up and get back to where you were," he said. "We'll start all over again."

Red in the face and feeling foolish, Hubert started for the sideline. As he did so, a low voice said, almost in his ear, "Just wait. I'll get you for this." The voice was almost a hiss.

5 The next day, to his surprise, Hubert found himself the
center of interest to a number of his schoolmates—and
something of a hero. The story of his spectacular catch and
his wrong-way run had made the rounds of the school. He
was pointed out amid a good deal of laughter and some
cheers. All this attention made him feel shy, but the laughter was good-natured and the applause couldn't help but be
flattering.

It didn't take him long to discover, however, that much of
the interest focused on him was because the pass he had
caught had been intended for George Tohatchi, a Navajo.
Frank explained it as, a few days later after classes, he and
Hubert walked across the Parade Ground to the dorm.

"Gee, kid," he said, chuckling, "you sure bought yourself a mess of trouble by catching that pass. George is going to have it in for you from now on. He should have caught that ball before it ever went out of bounds and you grabbed it. Now he thinks everybody is laughing at him. If I know George, he won't take it. He'll put the blame on you and get even with you if it's the last thing he ever does."

"I guess that's what he was trying to tell me," Hubert said, looking worried. "But I didn't mean to do anything to him."

"I know you didn't." Frank laid a reassuring arm across Hubert's shoulders. "But George is a Navajo—they're proud. And besides, a lot of them just plain don't like Hopis."

Hubert frowned. "Well, a lot of Hopis don't like Navajos much either," he said after a pause. "Many times they have tried to take away our lands. My grandfather and my father have told me."

"Sure, I know that," Frank answered. "But watch your step. I wouldn't get off into any dark corners if I were you!"

The two boys were halfway across the Parade Ground when a voice called out, "Hey! Wait up, you guys." A tall boy whom Hubert didn't know came running toward them. "You, Honanie," he said breathlessly, "you're supposed to show up for track tryouts—right now. Mr. Murdoch sent me to find you. He said you're to report on the double. He saw your wrong-way run the other day." The boy grinned and winked at Frank.

"Well, kid," Frank said, "I guess you better get going

with this Paiute here. His name's Ralph and he's our star quarter-miler. Good luck—and be sure you run the right way!"

Hubert wasn't quite sure what this track team was all about, but he followed Ralph at a quick jog to a big open space beyond the football field. Two dozen or more boys, dressed in white shorts and sleeveless white shirts, were clustered around a tall white man. The man nodded as Ralph and Hubert came up. "Okay, so you found him," he said to Ralph. "Take him to the locker room and get him into a track suit."

Like so much of what had been happening to him lately, this new experience was a bit confusing to Hubert, but once back on the field its purpose was plain enough—to run a race. To Hubert, it seemed funny to start the race by crouching down on all fours, feet back, fingertips just touching the ground. Out on the mesa you just started running. *"On your mark . . . Get set . . . GO!"* The first words meant nothing to him, but the word *Go* he knew. The three boys crouched on either side of him sprang into action—and so did Hubert.

Head up, chest lifted, arms pumping in rhythm with his bare legs, he gave no thought to the others alongside him. Once more he was back on the mesa, the wind in his face, the deep blue of the sky above him. He followed the oval track, rounded the curve . . .

At last he heard the sound of the white man's whistle. He slowed down and turned his head. He saw that the other boys had stopped running. They were heading back toward the white man who was waving a long arm in his direction.

"Come back here, Honanie!" the man called. "You're fast, all right," he said as Hubert jogged up to him. He looked him over carefully. "If you were only taller and had longer legs you'd make a great distance runner. But you'll do as a sprinter—in the 220 or maybe the 440. We'll try you out with the track team from now on. Report here for practice every Wednesday afternoon after classes."

Hubert hadn't the vaguest idea what the 220 or the 440 were, but he nodded his head. To run—he'd do anything Mr. Murdoch wanted, for that! Running, he could leave behind him, if even for a little while, this puzzling white man's world. He could forget its bells, its strange, tasteless food, the boys and girls who laughed at him when he made mistakes.

6 For Hubert the days passed quickly enough. His studies were hard but, almost without knowing it, he began to understand more and more of the white man's language and to speak it more easily. When one of his teachers asked him a question in class he was able to answer without stammering as he had done at first. He began to know and to like most of his classmates and the other boys in his dorm. His bunkmate, a Havasupai from Utah named Harold, was friendly. Though he was older and in an upper grade, the two had many things in common, particularly their dislike of Anglo food, most of all the despised hash which appeared on the dinner or lunch table with regularity several times a week.

In addition to the daily study periods, hours spent in preparing for the next day's lessons, there was also what was known as the Sherman Work Program. Hubert was introduced to it a few days after the beginning of the term. He learned that each student was automatically assigned to regular duty in some part of the school—helping in the kitchen; doing yard work such as weeding, raking leaves, and cutting grass; or performing various cleaning and maintenance chores inside the dormitories.

Hubert found himself assigned to regular hours in the kitchen. There he was expected to wash dishes and help prepare vegetables. The kitchen was a domain of mystery at first and the first day he dropped a stack of dinner plates. After a thorough tongue-lashing from the angry Anglo cook for breaking dishes, he was at pains to be more careful and soon learned to do efficiently whatever was expected of him.

As a part of the Work Program, assignments were handed out from time to time for day work on neighboring ranches. Depending on the season, there was plenty of fruit to be picked or hay to be harvested. The outside jobs were eagerly sought after, for they put money in one's pocket. One Saturday Hubert got a job picking walnuts. By nightfall his back was stiff and tired and his hands were stained by the walnut hulls, but he had the satisfaction of jingling several shiny half-dollars which were all his own.

He soon learned where these earnings were most often spent. The chief delight of Sherman students were the journeys into town on a Saturday or Sunday afternoon. The various stores presented all sorts of tempting things to buy, but almost everybody headed immediately for the ice cream shop which stood on a convenient corner just at the edge of the town. There one could sit at the marble-top counter and order (if one could afford it) a concoction called a sundae—three scoops of ice cream drenched in chocolate or fruit sauce and topped with whipped cream and chopped nuts. Less expensive but equally appetizing was the tangy, bubbly ice cream soda in a variety of flavors. The soda quickly captivated Hubert, particularly the chocolate kind. He wished he could earn enough money to buy this delectable white man's invention at least once a week!

So life at Sherman progressed. Frank continued to be Hubert's staunch friend, always ready with advice, though he often teased the younger boy and sometimes scolded him for being "dumb." Just as she had predicted, Hubert saw almost nothing of Janet. He would glimpse her now and then across the Parade Ground or in the dining hall. Sometimes she would notice him and wave airily, or even smile, but she never stopped to talk to him.

What he looked forward to, more and more as the days passed, was the weekly workout with the track team. He was now a full-fledged member and would be competing in track meets with other schools in the spring. The team was now in what was called "fall practice," where, he was told, the training was not nearly as tough as it would be in the spring.

Hubert soon learned that, by the coach's standard, speed

wasn't everything. There was something to be mastered called "form and style" and there were rules for each race. This bothered him greatly at first.

Hubert's wrong-way run on the football field had ceased to be food for jokes or conversation and seemed to be largely forgotten by everyone—everyone, that is, except George Tohatchi. The two boys' paths did not often cross, but if by chance Hubert happened to take the same route across the Parade Ground as the Navajo, George would stop and stare at him, scowling his fierce scowl.

One evening, when Hubert had finished supper and was coming out of the dining hall alone, a low voice reached him out of the darkness. "Be careful, Hopi, your time is coming," the voice said, just above a whisper. "Navajos don't forget insults."

Before Hubert could answer, or even quite take in the meaning of the words, he saw a slim figure, almost a shadow, glide away into the deeper shadows. In spite of himself, he shivered. He turned back toward the safety of the lighted hall.

He found Frank talking to a group of girls who were giggling at something he was telling them. A few minutes later the two boys were walking together toward the dorm. With Frank beside him, Hubert felt safe. But when he told the older boy of George's whispered threat, trying to make light of it in case Frank should think him a coward, Frank looked grave. He shook his head. "That's bad, kid," he said at last. "That one sure can hold a grudge! You better be on the lookout, like I told you. Stay out of dark corners!"

"But what can he do to me?" Hubert asked. "He'd be scared to try to kill me. He can't mean that."

"Yeah, but he could beat you up plenty, don't think he couldn't!" Frank was frowning. "The Anglos come down on you hard if you're caught fighting," he went on, "but old George wouldn't care about that. He'd fix it so he wouldn't be caught and you'd be the one to take the blame."

But nothing happened and Hubert came near to forgetting all about George Tohatchi. The Navajo seemed to have vanished from sight.

After study hour was over one Wednesday evening, Hubert decided to turn in early. Track practice that afternoon had been unusually long and strenuous and his muscles felt pleasantly tired. He was running the 220-yard dash now, coming in several lengths ahead of most of the other boys in that race. But he still hadn't mastered what Mr. Murdoch called "style" and often got a bawling out from the coach for his performance, especially at the starting line. He was thinking about this as he climbed the stairs and headed for his bunk on the sleeping porch. He had had the porch to himself for the past week, since Harold had been called home to Utah because of the illness of his father. Hubert wondered about him as he undressed and climbed into pajamas, the Anglo-style nightwear that still seemed strange to him. He liked the Havasupai boy and hoped he would come back soon. But once in bed, he forgot the track team and Harold and fell instantly asleep.

He was awakened suddenly by a strange sound. He

opened his eyes. The sleeping porch was in almost total darkness, lighted only by a dim glow that shone through the half-open door that led into the hallway.

Hubert sat up. What had wakened him? Then he saw. Looming above him was a face—a white face with red-rimmed eyes and a gaping red mouth. His Spirit Guide! He had known from early childhood about the Spirits who guided each Hopi through life but were almost never seen except at the point of death. He found himself in the clutch of a deadly fear. Was he about to die? *Why?*

Wide awake now, Hubert saw that the horrid grinning head had a body, dressed in a shirt and dark pants. Behind it were two other white-masked figures. The faces had the same red-rimmed eyes and grinning mouths.

In a low, muffled voice the first figure spoke. "Get up, Hopi coward," it said. "Your time has come!"

George—George Tohatchi! This was no Spirit Guide but a Navajo bent on revenge!

Hubert hit out blindly but his fist merely struck the air. Hands reached for him, fingers grasped his hair, pulling it hard.

"Come on, Hopi," the voice continued. "Come with us. You're going to get what you've been asking for."

"What—what are you doing? Where are you taking me?" In spite of himself, Hubert's voice was trembling.

"You'll find out soon enough," came the answer. George had pulled him out of the bunk and onto the floor. The two other figures were pinning his arms, crossing them behind his back and tying his wrists.

"Hurry up," one of the figures whispered. "The freight will be passing the crossing in the next hour. We haven't got much time!"

"Hear that, Hopi?" George's hand shot out, landing hard against Hubert's stomach. "We're going to throw you on that freight train when it slows at the crossing. Your feet will be tied so you can't jump off. By the time the sun comes up you'll be in the middle of the desert—*and you'll be plenty hot!* You'll die of thirst—and nobody will ever know what became of you!"

This *couldn't* be happening to him, Hubert thought wildly. He must be dreaming. If he yelled out he could wake himself up. He opened his mouth to yell, but instantly a hand closed over it and George's voice said in his ear, "No you don't! If you make a sound I'll choke you."

"Better gag him," a voice whispered. Cloth was being tied over his mouth and nose. It was hard to breathe.

"Let's get going—down the ladder the way we came up here." Two figures were moving to the open window at the porch railing. George shoved him in their direction. Just as he did so, there was a sound from the hall—footsteps, loud in the silence of the sleeping dormitory.

The Dorm Master, coming this way! At this time of night anyone but the Master would have crept along stealthily so as not to be heard. George held up a warning hand. The footsteps were slowing down, were almost at the door to the porch. In another instant, Hubert felt his hands being freed as the cord which bound them was jerked

48

off. The cloth covering his mouth and nose was suddenly pulled away. The two masked shapes at the window vanished; then Hubert saw George Tohatchi, his white mask clutched in his hand, disappear over the side. Silently, the open window closed.

Hubert turned to face the man standing in the doorway. His dark bulk was silhouetted against the light from the hall. "What goes on here?" a gruff voice demanded. "The boys next door heard a commotion in here and reported it. What are you doing out of bed? You're supposed to be asleep!" he added crossly.

"I'm sorry, sir," Hubert heard himself mumbling. The Master had flipped the switch which turned on the overhead light. Hubert saw the two boys from next door standing in the doorway, their eyes wide with curiosity.

"Get back to bed, you two," the Master told them sharply. "There's nothing here that concerns you. Now, young man," he said, turning back to Hubert. "Let's get to the bottom of this. What happened here just now? You'd better tell the truth if you know what's good for you."

Hubert thought, *Tell the truth—why not?* The whole frightening episode was not of his making. George Tohatchi deserved whatever punishment was coming, whatever fate lay in store for him at the white man's hands. It was not up to him to save the Navajo's hide at his own expense. *Tell the truth!*

Hubert opened his mouth to speak—but somehow the words did not come. Deep within him something seemed

49

to tie his tongue. *Hopis do not fight back, even when they are in the right . . . Hopis do not interfere with what another chooses to do . . .*

The Dorm Master was waiting. His face was very stern.

"Nothing happened, sir," Hubert mumbled. "I guess I had a bad dream. I—I'm sorry."

The Dorm Master continued to stare at him. At last he shook his head. "All right, Honanie," he said. "We'll see about this in the morning. You can tell the Superintendent all about it. Report to his office at 9 o'clock sharp. Perhaps by then you'll have a better story than a bad dream."

Back in bed, alone now in the darkness, Hubert lay thinking. He was still badly shaken. Had George and his companions really meant to take him to the railroad crossing, dump him like a sack of cornmeal onto a passing freight car? What was the Superintendent going to say to him in the morning? What would be his punishment for this bad thing which was not his fault? George Tohatchi was his enemy! Unbelievably, he had planned to do away with him. If Hubert did not report what had happened tonight here on the sleeping porch he, not George, would be punished.

After awhile Hubert fell into a troubled sleep.

7 The morning sun shone bright across the Parade
Ground. It was nearly deserted now. Breakfast had
long been over and almost everyone had gone to classes.
The clock in the outer office said 9:30 when Hubert walked
out of the low building which housed the Superintendent
and his staff. In his hand was the note he had been given
to excuse his lateness for his first class.

He walked slowly. The session with the Superintendent
had been less painful and frightening than he had feared.
The Dorm Master had been there too. He had begun by
telling how he had been awakened by Hubert's next-door
neighbors; how he had felt sure that something strange was

going on, out on the sleeping porch; how Hubert had refused to talk, claiming only that he'd had a bad dream.

When he had wakened early that morning Hubert had made up his mind to tell the whole story. Why should he protect George? The Navajo had been his enemy since the beginning, had taunted him, called him a Hopi coward. And last night he had tried to do him real harm, perhaps even kill him! Besides, if he did not see that George was brought to justice, the Navajo would go on tormenting him.

While the Dorm Master was speaking, Hubert tried to arrange his thoughts. Yes, he would tell these white men the whole miserable story, beginning with that first afternoon on the football field.

From behind his big desk the Superintendent was looking at him, waiting for him to speak. "Well, Hubert," he said, "let's have it. I want the truth now, remember."

Hubert swallowed hard. "It was only a bad dream, sir," he heard himself saying. "I guess I made a lot of noise before I woke up. I— I'm sorry, sir," he stammered.

Why had he answered as he had? With the toe of his shoe Hubert kicked a pebble from his path. What he had done was without reason, without sense even. He had no answer for his own question. He only knew that, standing there in that quiet office before the two white men, something out of the past, something age-old, had come welling up, making it impossible for him to give George Tohatchi away. *Hopis do not punish evil-doers. Only the gods can do that . . . Hopis do not interfere with others . . .* Was it Grandfather who had taught him these things?

52

The day seemed very long. Hubert stumbled through his classes, unable to give correct answers to any of the questions he was asked. After classes were over, he headed for the gym. He would work out by himself for an hour or so. Exercise on the bars always made him feel better.

It was growing dark when he set out for his dorm. He must wash up before the dinner bell rang. He had almost reached the dorm entrance when he heard a low whistle. He turned his head. Standing in the deep shadow of the building was George Tohatchi!

Hubert halted. He stood very still. "I want to talk to you, Honanie," George said.

"Go away!" Hubert answered sharply. "I don't want to talk to *you*—ever." He started to move on.

George stopped directly in his path. When he spoke, his voice was very low. "You didn't tell the Superintendent about last night. If you had, he would have clobbered me by now. Why didn't you tell?"

"I don't know. I *should* have told—you murderer! Stay away from me!" Hubert started to move on.

"Wait a minute! We weren't going to hurt you. I only wanted to scare you." George's voice was almost pleading. "I bribed those other two guys to help me. We thought those masks we made would shake you up and frighten the daylights out of you. But we weren't going to hurt you," he repeated.

"You mean—you weren't going to put me on that freight?" Hubert sounded amazed.

"Of course not! We never could have done it anyway,

even if we'd wanted to. We were going to take you outside and leave you tied up under a tree is all. If the guys next door hadn't heard us, we'd have gotten away with it too."

He paused. The two boys eyed each other. Then George said, "Thanks for not telling on me. You're an all-right guy, Honanie, even if you are a Hopi."

8 The days passed swiftly. They were growing shorter now, for winter was coming on. There were classes, study hours, the things called exams which Hubert dreaded. While he certainly did not excel in any school subject, he was no longer dismally behind the other boys and girls. He was speaking the Anglo language with readiness now, almost without thinking about it, and reading English with ease.

It was the white man's plan of education that, in addition to book learning and the Work Program, each Indian student should learn a trade, a skill by which, someday, he could earn a living in the white man's world. Hubert was assigned to the carpentry shop where he reported for several hours a week. He learned to use carpentry tools he had never heard of and soon began to turn out handsome objects. He was proud of his way with wood. Carpentry was far easier than civics or arithmetic!

And he was making great progress on the track team. He was not only running the 220 but the 440-yard dash as well. Not only his time, but his style, which had been such a stumbling block at first, had improved so much that Mr. Murdoch often praised him to the other runners. More than once he had thumped him on the back, a sure sign of approval.

But the most important thing in Hubert's life was his growing friendship with the Navajo, George Tohatchi. For several days following their encounter when George had apologized for what he had done, Hubert saw nothing more of him. Then suddenly, on a Sunday afternoon after the midday dinner when everybody had returned to their rooms for the customary Sunday rest period, George appeared in the doorway to the sleeping porch. He was grinning.

"Hi," he said. "If you're not doing anything, how about walking into town and having an ice cream soda? On me, I mean."

Hubert was so surprised that for a moment he didn't answer. He simply stared at George, wide-eyed. Then he too started to grin. "You bet," he said.

A few minutes later the two boys were walking down the palm-lined street that led into town. George explained that yesterday he had worked all day at a nearby dairy farm. He had earned three dollars, hence this unexpected treat. "You can have *two* sodas if you want to," he told Hubert. "I can afford it."

Hubert felt embarrassed. "One will be okay," he muttered. After that, they didn't say much. Finally, when Hubert asked where his home was, George said his family lived in Monument Valley, a part of the Navajo reservation in northern Arizona. This, he said, was his second year at Sherman.

Soon the two boys were perched on the high stools before the counter in the soda shop, pulling the bubbly sweet sodas through the paper tubes the white man behind the counter called straws. It was necessary to eat the ice cream and syrup at the bottom of the glass with a long-handled spoon. It tasted delicious. The last of the sodas made a satisfying gurgle when sucked through the straws.

Afterwards, they strolled along the sidewalk, looking in the windows of the downtown Riverside shops. As always, Hubert was amazed at the variety of things these Anglo stores had for sale. "Mostly junk," George said when Hubert commented.

Both boys were more talkative on the way back to school. They compared notes about their feelings for Sherman. George said that he had hated the school at first and once last year had made plans for running away. But he had been found out and punished. He hadn't tried again. Hubert confessed his own homesickness in those first weeks, but added that he liked things better now. He boasted a bit about his record on the track team. George told him of the upcoming football game with Riverside High School the following Saturday and voiced his hope that he'd be in the lineup at game time.

After lights out that night Hubert lay awake for a time, thinking about George. It didn't seem possible that his friendly host of the afternoon was the same boy who had waited for him in dark corners, had tied him up in this very room. He was more than glad now that he had refused to tell on the Navajo. He had never told anyone, not even Frank, about that scary night.

As the days passed, Hubert found he was spending more and more of his precious free time with George. When they could, the two boys took walks together, into town or across the brown countryside. They swapped accounts of life at home on the Hopi and Navajo reservations. Hubert was surprised to learn about the number of times George's family had moved, had built new houses called hogans—six-sided structures of wood covered with brush and layers of sod—so different from his own stone and adobe house at Chimopovy.

George explained that, like most Navajos, his father was a sheep owner and must often move to find new grass for his flocks. George had two younger sisters and a younger brother. They went to government day schools from time to time and would, he supposed, eventually come to Sherman when they were old enough. But by the time they did,

George would have graduated. He admitted that he missed his family and was sometimes homesick.

Hubert made a point of seeing as many of the Saturday afternoon football games as he could, whether or not George was scheduled to play. After the football season ended— Sherman won its last game against an unusually tough team, with George making the final touchdown—the Navajo often came to watch track practice. He admired Hubert's sprinting ability and told him so with enthusiasm.

The change in George, from the proud, silent, even sullen young Navajo to a boy who talked readily with other boys and girls, often volunteered to recite in class, and was generally cheerful and friendly, did not go unnoticed by his classmates as well as his instructors. George was beginning to be quite popular with both.

Although he gave it no thought and perhaps would not have understood the cause if he had, Hubert too was changing. George was never afraid of anything or anybody, as Hubert often was. George didn't hesitate to speak his mind whenever something or someone displeased him. Hubert, trained in the Hopi way of taking whatever came without complaining or fighting back, even when something was uncomfortable or unfair, marveled at George's fearlessness. Slowly, he began to gain more self-confidence and to lose some of his timidity.

Now Christmas was approaching, the white man's biggest celebration of the year. Of course, all the boys and girls at Sherman were supposed to celebrate it too.

Since entering Sherman, Hubert had gone on several Sundays with other boys and girls to a neighboring church, but, though he never said anything about it, he had not been very impressed with what he had seen and heard there. It seemed strange to him that the all-powerful Anglos worshipped only one God instead of several gods as the Indians did.

The week before Christmas the Superintendent issued an order that the whole student body was to attend church the Sunday preceding December twenty-fifth. Hubert listened very carefully to what the preacher said about the coming of the Baby Jesus, but he did not understand why the birthday of this Child was of such importance to the white man.

Christmas Day was fun, however. It was a holiday with no classes or study hour. And there was a special dinner for everybody at noon—turkey and cranberries and mince pie. Hubert would have preferred stewed rabbit or mutton and corn cooked in the Hopi way, but he ate two helpings nevertheless. After dinner there was a special assembly in the auditorium. The big hall was decorated with greens and red berries. On one end of the platform was a tall green tree hung with many colored balls and blazing with colored electric lights. A mixed chorus of boys and girls sang songs called Christmas carols. Hubert liked the music well enough, though the words meant little to him.

When the program was over and everyone was filing out of the auditorium onto the Parade Ground, Hubert found his sister Janet walking beside him. He hadn't talked to her in many weeks. When he saw her, usually at a distance, she was always surrounded by boys and girls her own age. Hubert thought she must be very popular with her classmates.

Janet was frowning at him as he fell into step beside her. She looked very cross. "What's this I hear about you and that Navajo boy?" she asked as soon as they were outside. "How come you have a Navajo for a friend?"

Hubert opened his mouth to answer, but Janet went on indignantly, "What would Grandfather say? Don't you know that Hopis and Navajos are enemies? Navajos have tried to take away our lands time after time! And for years they've been stealing our crops and even our sheep—"

"George doesn't know about things like that," Hubert retorted. "He's never stolen anything from anybody!"

"That's only because he hasn't had a chance then." Janet stamped her foot. "You better stop being friends with this George—or else." She turned on her heel and flounced off.

Angry thoughts welled up in Hubert. Janet was wrong! He wanted to run after her and tell her so, but she had disappeared in the crowd of students pouring from the auditorium. Before he could decide what to do he felt a hand on his arm. There stood George, grinning at him. The two boys had had dinner together but had gotten separated at the door of the auditorium before the program began and hadn't sat together.

"Hi," George said. "Was that your sister talking to you

just now? I'll bet she was giving you what-for, for being friends with a Navajo. Wasn't she?"

Hubert nodded dumbly. He felt miserable. George sighed. "Sure, I know," he said. "That was the old way. Navajos and Hopis hated each other for years. But we know better, even if your sister doesn't! Come on, I'll race you to the flagpole. And maybe I'll beat you too—you Hopi!"

9   After Christmas the rains came. It rained day after
day until the Parade Ground looked like a great shallow
pond. The track team met for exercises in the gym instead
of practice outdoors. Boys and girls sloshed their way to
classes and a general feeling of gloom hung over the entire
school. The Anglos called this the "rainy season" and com-
plained about it, but Hubert thought with envy how welcome such a season would be in his father's fields where it
rained so seldom.

Then the sun shone once more and the fields surrounding
the school began to turn a rich green. A yellow flower called
wild mustard sprang up everywhere. The days were gradu-

ally growing longer. Hubert and George took long hikes together, sometimes in the company of Frank or Hubert's bunkmate, Harold.

After his encounter with his sister Janet on Christmas night, when she had scolded him so roundly for making friends with a Navajo, Hubert decided that he would seek her out and set her straight about George Tohatchi. And, as he thought about doing so, he made a very pleasant discovery. He was no longer afraid of his sister Janet! He didn't care anymore what she might say to him. He didn't mind in the least, he told himself, that she had warned him never to bother her at school. What he had to tell her would be sure to make her mad. So what? Let her be mad. There was nothing she could do about it.

What he had to tell his sister was that he had invited George Tohatchi to come home with him to Chimopovy to spend as much of the coming summer vacation as he could.

The invitation had come about when he and George had been together one warm, lazy Saturday afternoon. The two boys had walked cross-country for several miles, then stopped to rest in the shade of a giant eucalyptus tree. As they often did, they talked of homes and families, comparing differences in their separate ways of life. George had never seen a kiva, did not even know what one was. Hubert described the three great underground chambers on the Second Mesa and told George about his initiation into the Kachina Cult and his disappointment at missing so many of the Kachina ceremonies which took place in the spring.

From George he learned that the Navajos held many dance ceremonies, but he gathered that they were very different from those performed by the Kachinas.

But it was not until Hubert mentioned the Snake Dance, the greatest of all Hopi religious ceremonies, that George's interest really came alive. He sat up suddenly. "Gee," he said, "I sure would like to see your Snake Dance! Do the priests *really* dance with live *rattlers* in their mouths? I've heard about that, but I never believed it."

Hubert hastened to assure him that this was so. As graphically as he could, he described how, four days before the Snake Ceremony began, the men of the village went out into the hills and the desert to collect the snakes, how they were then washed and purified with sacred cornmeal, how they became manageable and even harmless by being stroked with feather-tipped whips so that they would not coil to strike.

George was really excited now and repeated his wish to see the Snake Dance.

"Come ahead—come on home with me," Hubert said suddenly. "Then you can see for yourself. Lots of Navajos come to our Snake Ceremony."

The two boys could talk of nothing else for several days. George was writing his parents for permission to visit Hubert when the school term ended. Hubert would also write to his father, saying he was bringing home a guest. And he must tell Janet.

The meeting with her was less stormy than he had

feared. When he sought her out one afternoon at the end of classes, before she'd had time to head for her dorm or the girls' gym, she was plainly annoyed. She dismissed the girls she had been walking with by a wave of her hand and glared wrathfully at her brother.

"I told you never to bother me," she snapped.

A few months ago Hubert would have ducked his head and moved a pace backward. Now he held his ground and looked his sister full in the face. "I just wanted to tell you," he said, "that I've asked my friend George Tohatchi to come home with me for vacation. He'll be coming with us on the train to Flagstaff."

Of course Janet stormed. She flung some insulting Hopi names at Hubert, including a name which meant "traitor." She had even more insults for Navajos—all Navajos— and George Tohatchi in particular. At last she wound down, impressed, in spite of herself, with Hubert's firm stance and impassive face.

"Okay," she said, "bring on your friend." She hesitated, then added, "Besides, from what I hear, he really *is* a pretty nice guy, even if he is a Navajo."

10 Permission for George to visit Hubert's family at
Chimopovy came in a letter to the Superintendent
from George's father. George's railroad ticket to Flagstaff
and his bus fare to Monument Valley would be paid for by
the Government. Hubert's father had also sent word that
George would be welcome in the Honanie household. The
two boys were jubilant.

Spring was in full flower now and the most important
sports event of the season was about to take place. The
track meet, made up of teams from five competing schools,
four of them Anglo high schools, was set for the last Saturday afternoon in May. Track practice had been stepped up

to several afternoons a week and Hubert had been training extra-hard. He took his meals with his teammates at a training table in the dining hall. It had a special menu—lean beef, vegetables, and lots of milk. Hubert didn't care much for the food but he ate it all anyway. He'd do anything that would help him win the event he was down for.

He was to run the 440-yard dash. He'd speeded up his time and was feeling more and more sure he'd at least make a good showing, even if he didn't actually win the event. During the practice sessions Coach Murdoch drove his boys mercilessly. Some of them grumbled, but not Hubert. He still felt that wonderful sense of freedom whenever he ran —as though he could go on forever. The coach no longer scolded him for faults in style. He had really mastered that problem.

The day of the meet was clear and sunny and by one o'clock, time for the first event, it was hot. Almost the entire school had turned out. Boys and girls filled the bleachers alongside the oval track. As Hubert took his place on one of the benches reserved for his team he spotted George sitting as near to the starting line as possible. And there was Frank, halfway up in the bleachers. He had thought that Janet probably wouldn't come, for he knew she wasn't keen on sporting events. But there she was, surrounded, as always, by her friends. She saw him and waved.

The boys from the four white high schools all seemed very confident. They laughed and joked with each other. Probably some of their jokes had to do with their Indian competitors. Hubert didn't care. In sports Sherman was second to none among the schools in the county.

At last it was time for the sprints, the short-distance running. Hubert began warming up. He eyed the runners from the other schools. Most of them were taller than he was, with longer arms. He would have to concentrate all his thinking, all his will power, on keeping up his speed for the entire distance.

Now it was starting time. Hubert had drawn one of the longer outside lanes, which meant that he was given a start of four yards ahead of the runner on the inside lane next to him. He wished that he had had the luck to draw the very shortest inside lane.

But, at the sound of the starting gun, all worry disappeared. His start was fast. He was running as near as he could to the inside line of his lane, which would shorten his distance a little. Here came the turn. He leaned forward, just a bit, as he rounded it, then straightened. Now for the final hundred yards!

He was nose to nose with the runners on either side of him. In a great burst of speed, his leg muscles straining, his lungs struggling for air, he crossed the finish line. He had won!

For a few days Hubert basked in the warmth of the entire school's approval of his performance. He was told that his name would be engraved on the silver cup Sherman would be awarded for winning the most points in the meet.

He might well have gotten a swelled head from so much attention had he not quickly learned that fame is indeed fleeting. The meet faded swiftly into the past. The end of the school year was now in sight and final examinations were on everybody's minds. Also, there was Commencement Day to prepare for. The seniors in the high school division, the class of 1929, would get their diplomas and leave Sherman for good. A few of the graduates would go on to the white man's colleges. Others would seek jobs in the Anglo world. Many would simply return to their lives on the reservations.

For the rest of the school there was the suspense of not knowing whether or not one had passed from a lower grade to the grade above. And, before that, there was the strain of final tests in each subject to be gotten through. Hubert was beginning to worry. Suppose he didn't pass! Suppose he was stuck in the fifth grade for another whole year!

His showing in the tests was far from impressive, but he did get by. He received passing grades in all subjects and was on the list of promotions to grade six in the fall. Now he could settle down to enjoying Commencement Day and the prospect of the vacation which lay ahead. He was happy that George was coming home with him. Also, he would not have to say a real good-bye to Frank. The village of Oraibi where Frank came from was not far from Chimopovy and they laid plans to meet during the summer. Frank would, without fail, visit Chimopovy for the Snake Ceremony in late July.

The Commencement exercises passed off in a blaze of band music. Diplomas were handed out and the Superintendent and other faculty members made speeches. The speeches, mostly about the great opportunities that lay before the graduates out there in "Anglo land," meant little if anything to Hubert whose mind kept wandering to the trip home tomorrow and the weeks of freedom which lay ahead.

11   *"Flagstaff—Flagstaff, Arizona!"* the conductor was calling. Hubert sat up with a start. The train had slowed to a crawl. Out of the car window he could see the little railroad station coming into view. How many months had it been since he had first seen the station and the great puffing monster that stood beside it, ready to carry him away into a frightening new world? How different had been this return train trip! He had felt completely at ease with the train's trappings, even the gadgets in the men's room.

And there was his friend George beside him. The boys had talked away a good part of the night, not disturbing

Janet who slept curled up on a seat across the aisle. Before their journey began, Hubert had been very nervous about how Janet would treat George when they met. Would she be friendly? Or would she stick her nose in the air and pretend to be superior to the Navajo boy? Janet could be very uppity when she wanted to be.

But he need not have worried. He could tell, almost at once after he had introduced George, that Janet was impressed. Soon after they boarded the train she was talking away to George, more friendly than he had ever seen her.

Now they were in a car headed for Chimopovy. Mr. Downing, who had seen them off last September, had come to meet them. So much had happened to Hubert since that day! He wondered if it showed and if Mr. Downing thought him any different.

How dry the earth looked as the car sped along the desert road! How different was this land from the one he had just left. He thought almost wistfully of the green-leafed trees and the green grass of California. Now he could see the outline of the Three Mesas in the distance, Chimopovy perched atop the second one. Soon there were the fields his father and the other men of the village cultivated—the rows of corn, the bean and melon patches, the few fruit trees. And there was the one-room day school where he had spent the better part of four years. It looked so small!

When they reached the house on the mesa, his father, his sisters Rachel and Tirzah, and the little ones—Ernst, Kathleen, and Adella—were in the doorway to greet them. The three small children were wide-eyed and silent at meeting a stranger, but Hubert's father and the older sisters had words of welcome for George.

Hubert looked around him. This room with its fireplace, where the whole family ate and slept, somehow seemed darker, more cramped than he remembered it.

Soon it was time to eat the supper Rachel had cooked. How wonderful the Hopi food tasted after all those months of nothing but flat-tasting Anglo food! Hubert saw that George was eating with relish—at least two helpings of rabbit and squash, and heaps of piki bread.

Hubert's father explained that Grandfather had had to go early to the Antelope kiva. As chief of the Antelope Society, he was already directing preparations for the Antelope participation in the coming summer ceremonies. He would greet Hubert and his friend later on.

After supper Hubert and George went out of doors. The sun was going down and its last rays lighted the stony plaza with a reddish glow. To Hubert the flat-topped stone houses, built in terraces one above the other, looked just the same. A group of boys was spinning tops in the middle of the plaza. Farther along, a game of kick ball was in progress. People were calling to each other from the rooftops of their houses. Hubert explained that, during the hot-weather months, many families slept all night on their roofs to get away from the stuffiness indoors.

"We'll sleep out tonight," he told George. George laughed. "No bells to tell us when to go to bed—or when to get up either!" he said. "I'll like that!"

As the boys walked along they met a number of the village men. Many of them stopped to greet Hubert. Most of them spoke in Hopi and a few of the men called him by his Hopi name, Dawa-Wufto.

"Where are they all going?" George asked presently.

"To one of the kivas," Hubert answered. "They mostly go there evenings to smoke and talk. Right now the Kachinas are down there, getting ready for the Niman, the Home-Going Ceremony."

The boys had walked almost to the entrance of the Antelope kiva, that dim underground room reached by ladders. Hubert wished that he could show it to George, but of course all kivas were forbidden to outsiders.

George was curious about the Kachinas. "I've heard about them forever," he said. "I sure would like to see some of them."

"You'll see some tomorrow," Hubert assured him. "They start coming to our villages in December and they stay till July. In a few weeks they'll have their good-bye dance. Then they'll go back to the mountains to sleep in caves until winter. But before the Niman, the good-bye dance, they'll be around. Some of them will dance in the plaza for most of the day tomorrow."

George looked at Hubert out of the corner of his eye. "You don't *really* believe all that stuff, do you?" he asked. "I mean, that Kachinas are Spirits that carry messages to the gods, or something? Do you really think they bring rain and make the crops grow? And that they live in the mountains?"

Hubert hesitated, then grinned at George. "I used to believe all of it," he said finally. "If I tell you how it *really* is, you've got to promise *never* to let on to any of the kids in this village while you're here. Do you swear you won't tell?"

George raised his right arm. "I solemnly swear it," he said.

It was getting dark and the boys headed back toward Hubert's house. The village was growing quiet, the youngest ones already asleep. They dropped down in front of the doorway, sitting cross-legged.

"Well," Hubert began, "I really did believe that all the Kachinas were magic and stuff until I got initiated into the Kachinas Cult. As a member I could go into the kiva any time I wanted to when the Kachinas were there, even when they were getting ready for a big ceremony. Just before the spring Bean Dance, I went with Grandfather to see them. Boy, did I *ever* get a surprise! There they were, all dressed up—*but they didn't have their masks on.* They weren't Spirits—they were my father and my uncles and the village men I'd known all my life."

George began to laugh. "It wasn't funny then," Hubert told him ruefully. "I felt like someone had hit me and I wanted to bawl." But, he went on, Grandfather, seeing his disappointment, had explained it all very satisfactorily. When he had finished doing so, Hubert had felt very grown-up, very proud that he was now old enough to understand. In a way, each man *was* a Kachina, Grandfather had said. Each represented a certain individual Spirit-Messenger to carry the needs of the people to the gods. Each man chosen for this solemn task had a very important mission to perform. First, he must empty his heart and mind of all thoughts of himself. Then, and only then, could the spirit of the real Kachina work through him. With the putting on of each special mask and costume the transformation was supposed to take place.

As he talked, Hubert had been looking out over the mesa. Now he glanced quickly at George. He was more than a little afraid that his Navajo friend might think all this quite silly. But George's face was serious. "I understand," he said. "We are not far apart, we Navajos and Hopis. My people do not call them Kachinas, but we have something like them, at least a little. Ours are called Impersonators and they are said to be the bridge between men and the gods. I guess I believe that," he added.

12 The sun was just beginning to edge its way above the rim of the mesa when Hubert woke up. For a moment he did not know where he was. He opened one eye and saw George lying next to him, rolled up in the sheepskin he had been given the night before. There on the rooftop the air was sharp and clear. A little morning breeze ruffled George's black hair. Hubert pounced on the Navajo, pulling a lock of his hair. George woke up and for a moment the two boys tussled, rolling over each other on the flat rooftop.

Hubert jumped to his feet. "Come on, you lazy Navajo," he said challengingly. "I'll race you up to the spring. You need a good dunking in cold water to wake you up!"

The water felt icy as they splashed it on their faces and chests. "Cold water's good for you," Hubert said between chattering teeth. "That warm water the white man uses makes you soft and weak."

"Don't tell *me*," George answered. "My father rolled me in the snow every winter morning from the time I was six months old!"

The village was coming to life as they strolled back to Hubert's house. Women were shaking out blankets on the rooftops and hanging them over railings. Dogs were barking and naked small children had already begun to play in the plaza. In Chimopovy the day had started. To Hubert the scene was just as he remembered it. Nothing had changed. He had the feeling that he had never been away.

They found Rachel already busy preparing food for the Middle-of-the-Sun meal, which today would be a feast in honor of Hubert's homecoming. Most of the relatives would be there, including Hubert's favorite Uncle Thomas, his mother's brother, who now lived on his own farm down in the valley. Hubert's oldest brother Perry would try to make it all the way from Winslow where he had a job, Rachel reported. Of course, Grandfather would be sure to come, as would numerous aunts, uncles, and cousins who lived in the village. There would be quite a crowd. The house wouldn't hold them all. Some people would have to sit on the ground outside.

Rachel and Tirzah had been getting ready for the feast

for several days. Hubert's father had butchered a sheep in honor of the occasion, so there would be plenty of stewed mutton. Rachel was making Hubert's favorite *dosi*, a delicious corn pudding cooked in a special way. There would be ripe watermelons, and the piki bread Hubert had so missed.

Janet hurried the boys through their breakfast, shooing them out of doors as quickly as she could. "You two are only in the way here," she told them. "Go out and find the Mudheads. They'll be all over the place."

"What in the world are Mudheads?" George asked as they walked along.

Hubert chuckled. "You'll find out pretty soon," he answered. "It's too early in the day for any of them to be around."

The boys, followed by the three youngest Honanie children, walked down the trail that led to the fields below the mesa. They inspected the corn crop and Hubert told George, a bit boastfully, how he had helped his father plant corn when he was only seven years old. "It's the same with Navajos," George assured him. "I was in charge of herding sheep before I was ten."

On the way back to the village the boys planned a rabbit hunt for the next day. Hubert would lend George a bow and some arrows; he would use his old slingshot. When they reached the plaza a line of Kachina dancers in bright costumes was disappearing into one of the kivas. The plaza was crowded now with people who had been watching the performance. "Different Kachinas dance eight or nine times a day," Hubert said. He broke off suddenly, pointing. "Here come the Mudheads!" he shouted.

George gaped. A number of tall figures had appeared, seemingly out of nowhere. They all wore reddish-brown masks with two round, bulging circles for eyes. The masks were crowned by strange gourd-shaped objects at the sides and top. The figures sported bright neck scarves but otherwise were bare to the waist. Shabby black skirts, held in place by wide leather belts, completed their costumes.

The figures came on at a run. The grown people in the plaza began to laugh, but the children scattered, shrieking loudly. George soon saw why. One of the Mudheads reached out with a long arm, caught up a small boy who was in his path, and *snip!*—off went a lock of his hair. A minute later, George ducked—but not quickly enough to avoid the ball of soft mud which slid down the side of his neck.

When they were gone, vanishing as suddenly as they had come, Hubert explained that the Mudheads were the clowns—Kachinas on hand to entertain the crowds between the more serious ceremonies. They were full of mischief, but they never did any real harm.

The Middle-of-the-Sun feast passed off successfully. Hubert was a little nervous about how his relatives might receive George, a Navajo, but all went well. George was made to feel at home by everybody. Grandfather told him about several of his own Navajo friends, whom he valued highly, he said.

Most of the time, the guests spoke in the Hopi tongue but

when they remembered to include George in the talk, they courteously switched to English, the language which, except for the old people and the very young, everybody spoke. Hubert could tell that George made a good impression and he was proud of his friend.

13 The dry, hot summer days passed quickly. Hubert and George took long hikes on the desert, sometimes going as far as the mountains. In the village they joined with others in endless games—tag, kick ball, target-shooting with bow and arrow. Hubert showed George how to make whipping tops from soft cottonwood and how to whip them with string to make them spin. George soon learned to do this as expertly as the Hopi boys.

And always there were the Kachinas. Throughout each day they appeared, most of the time carrying presents to the delighted children who constantly hovered about the plaza, holding out grubby hands. There were dolls for the girls, gaily painted rattles and bows and arrows for the boys, and sticky candy for everybody.

Hubert's little sister Adella, who had taken a great liking to George and followed him about whenever she could, shyly showed him the doll she had been given. It was a Hemis Kachina, she said, and must be treated very, very carefully. She would be allowed to carry it with her sometimes but she must always hang it back on a special nail in the wall where it would stay most of the time.

George thought the doll strange but quite beautiful. It was a small painted wooden figure which wore a mask, with a headdress rising high above it in tiers. Its costume was blue, outlined in red and covered with a painted design. Around its neck was a green ruff.

"That's a Hemis Kachina all right," Hubert said, looking at the doll critically. "The Hemis is chief of the Home-Going Ceremony. He looks exactly like that—you'll see. Mind you take good care of him," he added to Adella.

The Niman, the Home-Going Ceremony, was just a few days off. Hubert had to leave George now and then in order to get ready for it. As a member of the Kachina Cult, he would be one of the masked dancers. He had always loved to dance and had long ago learned the basic Kachina dance step, the stamping of the foot in time to chanted music. Now he would be able to show George as well as his family how good a performer he was.

The day of the Kachinas' departure dawned bright and

84

hot under the fierce July sun. To George, watching from the housetop, the ceremony was full of wonder. As the Kachinas danced, he couldn't be sure which one of the moving figures was his friend Hubert. All wore masks like the one on Adella's doll, but the ruffs around their necks were made of live spruce branches.

From time to time the Kachinas paused long enough to give gifts, first to the children, then to the women crowding the plaza—dolls, rattles, quantities of food. By early evening they were ready to leave. A long line of them walked in dignified single file, out of the plaza, down the narrow trail from the mesa, until they were only black silhouettes outlined against the setting sun.

A few days after the departure of the Kachinas, preparations got underway for the greatest celebration of the year, the Snake Ceremony. It would last for nine days altogether and would end with the famous Snake Dance on the last day. Both Hubert and George were excited about it, though their enthusiasm was somewhat dampened by the knowledge that the ceremony would mark the end of George's visit. He would leave the day after for Monument Valley and home. One of Hubert's cousins, who owned a car, would drive him to Flagstaff to catch his bus. But they were cheered by the thought of the wonderful feast which would take place after the dance. And Frank would be with them. He had promised to come to Chimopovy in the early morning and to stay overnight.

"It's sure to rain after the Snake Dance," Hubert told George.

"Yeah?" George sounded skeptical. "It hasn't rained yet —not all summer."

"That's what the Snake Dance is for, dummy," Hubert retorted. "The snakes carry the message that Hopis need rain to the gods in the underworld. We always get a big rain afterwards. Okay," he ended, "laugh away if you want to. But you won't laugh when you get plenty wet!"

Hubert told George a little about the ceremonial preparations going on in the Snake and Antelope kivas, though of course he couldn't describe the secret ones. These were known only to the Snake and Antelope priests. George was most interested to learn how the snakes were gathered for the Snake Dance. This year, because of the presence of his guest, Hubert was not going to take part in the snake hunt, though he had done so several times in the past, even when he was only a small boy. He described to George how, four days before the dance, men and boys went out at dawn, across the desert to the hills. They would be armed with their snake whips, the long sticks tipped with feathers, to capture kingsnakes, gopher snakes, garter snakes, and, of course, the deadly rattlers.

"But rattlesnakes bite and their venom is poison," George objected.

"Nobody's been bitten yet," Hubert said proudly. "Even young kids know how to handle a rattler. You stroke him with the feathers on your whip so that he doesn't coil and strike—then you grab him right behind his head. That way he can't turn his head and bite you." George shuddered.

The secret preparations for the great ceremony went on in the kivas from dawn until far into the night. The Snake priests would be assisted by priests of the Antelope Society.

On the day of the Snake Dance the two boys were up before sunrise. They were too excited to sleep. The whole village seemed to be astir, alive with a holiday feeling. And Hubert and George were eager for Frank's arrival.

By midmorning the plaza began to fill with visitors— Hopis from other villages, Navajos from nearby, Anglo men, women, and children from as far away as Flagstaff and Winslow, cross-country motorists stopping off to see this most famous of all Indian rituals. Some Navajos came on horseback up the trail to the village. As always, they sat proudly in the saddle. Most of them wore the handsome turquoise and silver jewelry for which they were famous.

By midafternoon every possible outdoor spot in the village was occupied. The rooftops were packed with people. Hubert, George, and Frank had staked out a good spot well up in front of the crowd. From where they stood they had a fine view of the *kisi*, the leafy shrine made of green cottonwood boughs which would soon house the writhing, twisting snakes.

"Look!" Hubert cried excitedly. "There's the Antelope priest with the snake bag!" Out of one of the kivas came a tall figure carrying a bulging leather bag which rippled with the movement of its hidden contents. He walked through the entrance to the *kisi* and disappeared from sight.

Then, from the Antelope kiva, came an awesome procession—ten priests dressed in white kilts, their necks and arms encircled with heavy silver and turquoise ornaments, eagle feathers in their long black hair. A strip of white paint across each mouth contrasted sharply with the black paint on the chin. The long zigzag white lines on chests, backs, and arms represented lightning, Frank told George in a whisper.

The priests circled the plaza four times, their clappers of tortoiseshell fixed to their right knees, and their pebble-filled hand rattles making a strange, low accompaniment to their movements. Now each man filed past the *kisi*, stopping before the *saipu*, the shallow trench dug in front of the *kisi*, covered by a board. In the ceremonial tradition it represented the entrance to the underworld. On this cover each man stamped, at the same time reciting a low, strange-sounding chant. "They're asking the gods to hear their prayers for rain," Hubert whispered to George.

The Antelope priests were lining up now in front of the *kisi*. The line swayed gently. Then, out of their kiva came the Snake priests. They were dressed and painted like the Antelope men but they carried feather-tipped snake whips instead of rattles. They too circled the plaza four times, stamping on the *saipu* as an announcement to the underworld that the dance was about to begin.

88

Now Antelope and Snake priests faced each other in two lines and began their chant. The sound, low at first, rose in intensity. The lines swayed from side to side, the rattles of the Antelope priests and the whips of the Snake men keeping time with the rhythm of the chant.

Suddenly, in a swift, leaping movement, the line of Snake men broke up. The Antelope line parted and a Snake priest walked into the *kisi*. He came out almost instantly, a long snake held between his teeth. Another priest stepped directly behind him. In his right hand was the snake whip with which to stroke the snake should it show signs of the dangerous coiling.

Dancing in unison, the two men circled the plaza, keeping time with the Antelope priests' chant. Other pairs of dancers followed, until the circle was complete. When it was, the dancers dropped the snakes from their mouths. Then the gatherers, men who had accompanied each dancing couple, following along behind, swooped down to retrieve the reptiles and to return them to the *kisi*. Each time this was done, new snakes replaced those already danced with—on and on, until all the snakes were accounted for.

Now the chief priest stepped forward to make a great circle of sacred cornmeal upon the ground. Then the gatherers cast the snakes, a huge writhing mass of them, into the center of the circle. From the sidelines, women and girls, wearing white ceremonial mantles, advanced in a line to scatter meal on the wriggling pile.

This act marked the end of the ceremony. As the women

and girls drew back, the Snake priests rushed to the circle, plunged their arms into the snake pile, and emerged, each man with an armload of snakes, as many as he could carry. The crowd parted, making a path for the priests. Bearing their strange burdens, they ran down the trail from the mesa to the desert below. There they would scatter in all directions, releasing the snakes, their sacred messengers, to take word to the gods of the underworld that the Hopis of Arizona needed rain.

The sun had gone down but streaks of red still laced the dark bank of clouds slowly building up in the west. "It'll rain tonight all right," Hubert said, grinning at George.

The Navajo boy shook his head wonderingly. "You win! Not a cloud in the sky all summer until now. I guess the Snake Dance really *does* work."

Hubert and George and Frank were sitting cross-legged on the roof of Hubert's house, enjoying the cool of early evening. They had eaten their fill of the special food which all the women of the village had spent many days in preparing. They hadn't talked much, each thinking his own thoughts. In the minds of all three was the knowledge that, with the Snake Ceremony, vacation was drawing to its close. Soon each of them would be back in the world of the white man, trying once more to learn the white man's way of life.

"Frank, what are you going to do when you get out of Sherman?" Hubert asked after awhile.

Frank didn't answer at once. At last he said slowly, "I'll be darned if I know. Guess I'll have to be making up my mind pretty soon though. I've only got one more year to go."

"Do you want to come back and live on your reservation?" George asked.

Frank shrugged his shoulders. "I don't know. I don't want to be a farmer like my father. I'm not much good at farming. Fact is, I don't know *what* I'm good at."

"They make you learn stuff in school, like carpentry and metalwork, so you can get a job with the Anglos," Hubert said.

Frank nodded. "Yeah, I know. I'm learning metalwork in the school shop three days a week. But what chance would I have of getting a metalworker's job in one of those big Anglo cities where the good jobs are? A white man would beat me to it every time."

Hubert sighed. "All year I've been wishing I could finish school in a big hurry and get back here to live for the rest of my life. But now I don't know. It all looks—well—so small . . ." His voice trailed off.

"It's funny, isn't it?" George said. "They try to teach us how to be white men, but mostly the stuff we learn from their books and all does us as much good as a hole in the head—especially if we go back to our reservations. And unless we're real smart and get to go to college on a scholarship or something, we don't get enough education to really fit in with Anglos. It sure is a puzzle!"

The boys fell silent, watching the black clouds. They were moving toward them with greater speed now. Suddenly a jagged flash of light cut across them, followed by the sound of distant thunder.

Hubert stood up. "It'll be a real storm any minute now. And won't that old rain feel good!" He began to laugh. "I guess those Anglos we're talking about aren't really as smart as they think they are," he said. "Maybe they *know* more than we do—but who ever heard of an Anglo who could do a Snake Dance without getting bitten—*and make it rain?*"

A Selected Bibliography

Annixter, Jane. *The White Shell Horse.* New York: Holiday House, 1971.

Ceram, C. W. *The First Americans: A Story of North American Archaeology.* New York: Harcourt Brace Jovanovich, 1971.

Colton, Harold S. *Hopi Kachina Dolls.* Albuquerque: University of New Mexico Press, 1949.

Crane, Leo. *Indians of the Enchanted Desert, Arizona.* Boston: Little, Brown, 1925.

Curtis, Edward S. *The Hopi.* The North American Indian, Being a Series of Volumes Picturing and Describing the Indians of the U.S. and Alaska, vol. 12. Cambridge, Mass.: Cambridge University Press, 1922.

De Mente, Boye. *Visitors Guide to Arizona Indian Reservations.* Phoenix, Ariz.: Phoenix Books, 1976.

Dennis, Wayne. *The Hopi Child.* New York: John Wiley & Sons, 1940.

Dockstader, Frederick J. *The Kachina and the White Man.* Bulletin 35. Bloomfield Hills, Mich.: Cranbrook Institute of Science, 1954.

Ellis, Richard, ed. *The Western American Indian.* Case Studies in Tribal History. Lincoln, Neb.: University of Nebraska Press, 1972.

Embry, Margaret. *Shadi.* New York: Holiday House, 1971.

Forrest, Earle R. *Snake Dance of the Hopi Indians.* Arcadia, Calif.: Westernlore Press, 1961.

Furgusson, Erna. *Dancing Gods.* New York: Alfred A. Knopf, 1931.

Hanauer, Elsie V. *A Book of Kachina Effigies.* New York: A. S. Barnes, 1970.

Hodge, Gene Meany. *The Kachinas Are Coming.* Los Angeles: Stellar-Millar, 1936.

Hoffman, Charles. *American Indians Sing.* New York: The John Day Co., 1967

James, George Wharton. *Indians of the Painted Desert Region: Hopis, Navahoes, Wallapais, Havasupais.* Boston: Little, Brown, 1903.

James, Harry C. *The Hopi Indians.* Caldwell, Idaho: The Caxton Printers, 1956.

————. *Pages from Hopi History.* Tucson: University of Arizona Press, 1974.

————. *Red Man—White Man.* San Antonio: Naylor Company, 1957.

Jones, Louis T. *Amerindian Education.* San Antonio: Naylor Company, 1972.

Lavine, Sigmund A. *The Games the Indians Played.* New York: Dodd, Mead & Company, 1974.

Martin, Paul, and Plog, Fred. *The Archaeology of Arizona.* Published for The American Museum of Natural History. Garden City, N.Y.: Doubleday/Natural History Press, 1973.

Nequatewa, Edmund. *Truth of a Hopi.* Flagstaff: Northland Press, 1967.

Officer, James E. *Indians in School.* Tucson: University of Arizona Press, 1956.

O'Kane, Walter C. *Hopis: Portrait of a Desert People.* Norman: University of Oklahoma Press, 1953.

Sando, Joe S. *Pueblo Indians.* San Francisco: Indian Historian Press, 1976.

Silverberg, Robert. *The Pueblo Revolt.* New York: Weybright & Talley, 1970.

Simmons, Leo W. *Sun Chief.* New Haven: Yale University Press, 1971.

Simpson, Ruth De Ette. *Hopi Indians.* Los Angeles: Southwest Museum, 1953.

Stephen, Alexander M. *Hopi Journals,* 2 vols. Edited by Elsie C. Parsons. (Columbia University Contributions to Anthropology Series, vol. 23.) New York: Columbia University Press, 1936.

Thompson, Laura. *Culture in Crisis.* New York: Harper & Brothers, 1950.

Titiev, Mischa. *Hopi Indians of Old Oraibi.* Ann Arbor: University of Michigan Press, 1972.

Vroman, Adams Clark. *Photographer of the Southwest*. Los Angeles: Ward Ritchie Press, 1961.

Waters, Frank. *Book of the Hopi*. New York: The Viking Press, 1963.

————. *Masked Gods*. Sage Books. Chicago: Swallow Press, 1950.

Watkins, Frances E. *The Navahoes*. Los Angeles: Southwest Museum, 1973.

Wells, Robert N. "Clash of Cultures." Report on Higher Education. Canton, N. Y.: St. Lawrence University, 1972.

Wondriska, William. *The Stop*. New York: Holt, Rinehart & Winston, 1972.

Wright, Barton. *Hopi Kachinas*. Flagstaff: Northland Press, 1977.

————. *Kachinas: A Hopi Artist's Documentary*. Flagstaff: Northland Press, 1973.

MARJORIE THAYER, a native Californian, grew up on an orange ranch in Los Angeles County. After graduating from the University of California at Berkeley, she set out for New York and the world of book publishing. She was promotion manager of Alfred A. Knopf's juvenile department for a number of years, then went to Prentice-Hall where she organized and directed that firm's first children's book department. In 1962, she returned to the West Coast to edit Golden Gate Junior Books. She is the author of several plays for children and *The Christmas Strangers,* illustrated by Don Freeman. She makes her home in Hollywood.

British-born ELIZABETH EMANUEL grew up in London where she managed a bookshop. In 1951 she came to New York to join the Doubleday Bookshops, later becoming assistant children's book editor of Doubleday's Garden City division. In 1960 she moved to California, became a U.S. citizen, and settled in Hollywood. For many years she has been an independent researcher for the motion picture industry, associated particularly with Twentieth-Century-Fox. She has researched films such as *The Towering Inferno, Voyage to the Bottom of the Sea,* and *The Poseidon Adventure.* She has written documentary film strips and is the author of a children's book, *Baby Baboon.*

ANNE SIBERELL is an award-winning artist known for her woodcuts and prints, which have been exhibited in solo and group shows throughout the United States and also abroad. She is the illustrator and designer of distinguished children's books, including Mark Taylor's *Lamb, Said the Lion, I Am Here* and her own book, *Houses.* Mrs. Siberell received her art training at UCLA and the Chouinard Art Institute. She now lives in Hillsborough near San Francisco with her husband and three sons.